Acknowledgment

Many thanks to my wife, Kay, for her help with this book

Dedication

For my grandchildren.

Sky The SpaceCat

SKY was a very worried SpaceCat and there was a grave reason for it. Totally exhausted, she had just collected a cargo of canned fish to take back to her home planet from their sister planet, Felis.

Her home world, Felinia, had been overfished by its population of hungry cats and there was a short-age of food. Her family, friends, and neighbours were now living with hardly any food, with the waters almost empty of any life.

Sky was the Captain of her cargo
spaceship 'With Paws' and was now the only crew
member. Her old crew had
decided to settle on planet Felis where fish stocks
were bountiful and there were no food shortages.
The cats of Felis lived a happy life, as they slept
with their tummies full of delicious fish that filled
their oceans.

Sky found it quite difficult to pilot the ship on her own; looking after navigation, seeing to life support system warning bleeps and flying her ship without a co-pilot. Yet, she wasn't the kind to give up; Sky was one of the brave ones. She took it upon herself to save her planet from starvation, even when many chose an easier way out, as half of the population had decided to move to Felis.

Fortunately, Felinia was not too far from planet Felis, only four hours by Hypercat Drive. Sky still had to make sure she didn't hit any asteroids, planets, and bits of space-junk that littered the route between Felinia and Felis.

Sky found it quite difficult to pilot the ship on her own; looking after navigation, seeing to life support system warning bleeps and flying her ship without a co-pilot. Yet, she wasn't the kind to give up; Sky was one of the brave ones. She took it upon herself to save her planet from starvation, even when many chose an easier way out, as half of the population had decided to move to Felis.

Fortunately, Felinia was not too far from planet Felis, only four hours by Hypercat Drive. Sky still had to make sure she didn't hit any asteroids, planets, and bits of space-junk that littered the route between Felinia and Felis.

With parents who had served in the SpaceCat Force, Sky had grown up hearing horrifying stories of spaceships crashing into space junk or passengers being attacked by vicious alien beings, but even that didn't put a stop to her mission. After watching her loved ones going days without food, she'd had enough and decided to take matters into her own paws.

Sky felt relief washing over her as she realized she was close to landing on her home planet. A cheerful smile appeared on her face as she imagined the glee on her loved ones' faces as they would have a full meal after a very long time.

However, her happy thoughts were suddenly interrupted by a worried voice coming out of her radio. "Help! We are under attack!"

It took a while for Sky to realize that it was a distress call from another cargo ship, the 'With Whiskers', which was being attacked by Space Eels. This ship had broken down near a group of asteroids where a number of these very nasty creatures lived. They had wrapped themselves around the ship, slowly squeezing and electrocuting it. The Space Eels were well known for their attacks; they would target cargo ships more than the others as they lacked proper
protection against alien invaders.

This time, they were after the fish eggs the 'With Whiskers' was carrying to Felinia to try and re-stock the planet's oceans with fish. These eggs were a delicacy to the Space Eels.

Sky stopped her Hypercat Drive and fired the 'With Paws' thrusters so she could stop the ship near the 'With Whiskers' to drive away the Space Eels. She fired a low level pulse from special large white energy beam cannons that were fitted to both sides of the front of the 'With Paws'.

The power of the pulses only affected the Space Eels, and not the cargo ship they were leeching on furiously. They paralysed the electric current running through the Space Eels causing them headaches, which sucked away all their energy.

Being cowardly by nature, the Space Eels quickly freed themselves from the 'With Whiskers' and slunk away to a nearby
asteroid where they hid behind rocks, occasionally peeping around them to stare at the crews of both SpaceCat ships.

The 'With Whiskers' had been badly damaged by the squeezing of the Space Eels and was leaking a great deal of air. The Captain of the ship, Jarvis Moon, managed to seal the hold of his ship where the cargo of fish eggs was held, however, the crews' quarters had been badly damaged and needed some quick repairs before all the air leaked out.

Sky's radio had a voice again, but this time, it was deep and relieved. "'With Paws', thank you! You saved us. This is Jarvis Moon, the captain of 'With Whiskers'. Can you hear us? Over...."

Sky grinned ear to ear after hearing that the crew of the 'With Whiskers' was safe and sound. "The pleasure is mine, Captain Jarvis. This is Sky, the Captain of SpaceCat ship 'With Paws' speaking. What is the damage to your ship? Over ...."

"There is a great deal of damage to my ship, Captain Sky. Would you mind if my crew transfers to your ship? I am afraid the 'With Whiskers' cannot hold air much longer as it is rapidly leaking. Over...." Jarvis started pacing, anxiously waiting for Sky to answer.

"Please do so, Captain! I am opening the airlock doors. Start with the transfer right away. Over and out!" Sky called out with worry laced in her tone.

Luckily, the crew of 'With Whiskers', Captain and pilot Jarvis Moon, co-pilot Belle, SpaceCat engineers, Poppy and Charlie, and navigator Wilson already had their SpaceCat suits on.

A tube was attached between the two stationary SpaceCat ships and all the crew in the 'With Whiskers' raced along it to the 'With Paws' as quickly as they could.

Once all the SpaceCats had been strapped into all the spare seats on the 'With Paws', Sky set a course for Felinia, using the escape tube to tow the 'With Whiskers' slowly through space to safety.

When the two SpaceCat ships landed on Felinia, Captain Jarvis Moon found that the 'With Whiskers', was too badly damaged to be repaired. "What shall I do?" Jarvis asked Sky as they looked at the damage to the ship caused by the nasty Space Eels.

"I have a great idea." Sky's eyes glittered with excitement. "Sell your ship to the SpaceCat junkyard and let us join teams. Together, we can bring back the lost glory of Felinia. What do you think?"

Jarvis, after a little thought, nodded his head, echoing Sky's glee.

"Our next mission is to take a full cargo of waste that's been polluting our oceans to planet Rodentia!!" exclaimed Sky. "The rats and mice who live there don't like us cats, but they find our waste really yummy".

Jarvis laughed and glanced at his determined looking crew. With a beaming smile, he 'high-fived' Sky
and said, "We will be happy to join you, Captain
Sky...... Lead on!!"

The End

Printed in the USA
CPSIA information can be obtained
at www.ICGtesting.com
CBHW080104260624
10675CB00012B/952

9 781962 380713